Ava, the One and Only

LITTLE SIMON INSPIRATIONS

An imprint of Simon & Schuster Children's Publishing Division

1230 Avenue of the Americas, New York, New York 10020

Text copyright © 2005 by Karen Hill

Illustrations copyright © 2005 by Maryn Roos

All rights reserved, including the right of reproduction

in whole or in part in any form.

LITTLE SIMON INSPIRATIONS and associated colophon

are trademarks of Simon & Schuster, Inc.

Manufactured in the United States of America

First Edition

2 4 6 8 10 9 7 5 3 1

ISBN 1-4169-0511-1

Scriptures quoted from *The International Children's Bible*,

New Century Version, copyright © 1986, 1988

by Word Publishing, Dallas, Texas 75039.

Used by permission.

Ava, the One and Only

By Karen Hill

Illustrated by Maryn Roos

LITTLE SIMON INSPIRATIONS

New York   London   Toronto   Sydney

For the one and only
Caitlin Campbell Hill—I love you!
—K. H.

For LeAnn,
my fellow freckled friend
—M. R.

"God does not see the same way people see.

People look at the outside of a person,

but the Lord looks at the heart."

(I Sam. 16: 7)

Ava was a special girl. She had long red pigtails and floppy bangs.

She had a big smile. And she had . . . freckles!

Lots and lots of freckles.

Freckles on her nose.

Freckles on her cheeks.

She even had freckles on her toes.

Mom didn't have freckles. Dad didn't have them. Her big brother didn't have them. Only Ava.

Often Ava would ask her parents about her freckles.

"Why me?" she would ask.

Ava's dad would say, "You are the one and only Ava! There's not another like you in the whole world."

Mom would say, "We love you just the way
God made you, freckles and all. When you look
at your freckles, remember that God loves you."

Ava was proud of her freckles.

Until . . . Edith Louisa came along. In kindergarten class Edith Louisa always wanted to be the line leader.

At story time she always wanted to sit next to the teacher.

At show-and-tell Edith Louisa always said hers was the best.

And Edith Louisa did not like Ava's freckles.
"You have dirt on your face!" she would say,
laughing and pointing to Ava's freckled nose.
The other kids would laugh too.

Ava's dad said, "Just be kind to Edith Louisa. One day she'll learn to be your friend."

So Ava tried. During story time she sat beside Edith Louisa.

"You can't sit here, Spot Face!" Edith Louisa shrieked.

Ava didn't like being called Spot Face.

"Try again," said Dad.

So Ava tried again. The next day she tried to share her lunch with Edith Louisa. "Want a bite of my Krispy Krunchy Bar?" asked Ava.

Edith Louisa scowled. "No. I might catch your spots, Polka-Dot Girl!"

Ava's smile disappeared. She felt little warm
tears at the edges of her eyes. She couldn't wait
to get home and into the arms of her mom
and dad.

That night Ava cried to her parents, "I wish
I could paint my face and cover up all these
freckles."

Mom said, "You are the one and only Ava. You are just the way God wanted you to be. There's not another like you in the whole world."

The next day Ava's tummy felt like it had a jumping bean inside. "I don't want to go to

school," she told her parents.

"I think you don't want to see Edith Louisa,"
Dad said. "Just keep being kind. One day she'll
be kind to you, too."

So off Ava went to school.

As she put her lunch box in her cubby, Ava heard laughter. "Look at her! Ha, ha! She looks silly. . . ."

"Oh, no," Ava said to herself. "Not again."

Then she remembered her dad's words, "Just try . . . be kind."

Ava said a little prayer and asked God to help
her be kind . . . and *brave*.

She turned and headed toward the laughter.
A group of students were standing in a circle.
In the middle of the circle was . . . Edith Louisa!
She was wearing big, round, black glasses!

"Hey, Spider Eyes!" one of the kids called to
Edith Louisa. Edith Louisa's lip trembled. Her
eyes got watery. Ava walked right over to her.

"I think your glasses are pretty, and they make you look smart," Ava said, smiling.

Edith Louisa smiled too. "Thanks, Ava. I'm sorry I was mean to you before. Can we be friends now?"

"Positively!" Ava said. "We can all be friends," she said to the other kids. "It doesn't matter who has glasses or freckles or curly hair or big feet. We're all just the way God wanted us to be."

The morning bell rang.

"You know," Ava said to Edith Louisa as they walked to class together, "you're the one and only Edith Louisa. There's not another like you in the whole world. . . ."